The Ultimate Hunger Games Quiz Book

500 Questions for Hunger Games Lovers Everywhere

Mike Godfrey

Copyright © 2023 Nevno Publishing.

All rights reserved. This book or any portion thereof may not be reproduced or used in any manner whatsoever without the express written permission of the publisher except for the use of brief quotations in a book review.

Printed by Nevno Publishing, in the United Kingdom.

First printing, 2023.

The Ultimate Hunger Games Quiz Book

500 Questions for Hunger Games Lovers Everywhere

By
Mike Godfrey

Welcome to the ultimate Hunger Games quiz book.

In this book you are going to find 500 questions about the books and film versions of the Hunger Games, split into 25 separate rounds. You have the chance to test your knowledge and memory, and the questions cover a wide range of topics, including characters, actors, plot points, and general trivia.

The rounds are not split into themes, meaning that each round provides a random mix of trivia to test your knowledge. There is also a mix of difficulty, so this book will really test how much of a Hunger Games buff you actually are. The book is interesting and informative and will provide hours of fun for the most passionate Hunger Games fans everywhere.

Good luck...

Round 1

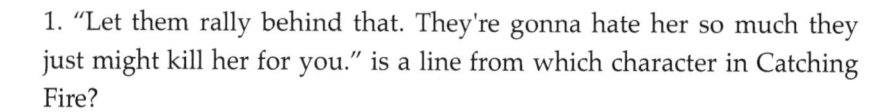

1. "Let them rally behind that. They're gonna hate her so much they just might kill her for you." is a line from which character in Catching Fire?

a. Plutarch

b. President Snow

c. Primrose Everdeen

d. Haymitch

2. What role is Plutarch Heavensbee given in Catching Fire?

a. Ceremonies Chief

b. Master of War

c. Head Gamekeeper

d. Lord Gamesman

3. Where is Peeta being tortured in "Mockingjay"?

a. District 2

b. District 12

c. Capitol

d. District 7

4. President Coin is the leader of which district?

a. 9

b. 13

c. 6

d. 3

5. Who led Panem after the War?

a. Commander Saylor

b. Commander Taylor

c. Commander Faylor

d. Commander Paylor

6. What age is it stated Finnick Odair was when he won The Hunger Games?

a. 17

b. 14

c. 21

d. 32

7. Haymitch won which version of the Hunger Games?

a. 50th

b. 70th

c. 1st

d. 5th

8. Chaff was a Hunger Games victor from which District?

a. 11

b. 3

c. 4

d. 6

9. How many boys compete in The Hunger Games events?

a. 12

b. 21

c. 31

d. 71

10. Who does Katniss pretend is her cousin to avoid his murder?

a. Gale

b. Woof

c. President Snow

d. Gale

11. Which character is turned into an Avox?

a. Gale

b. Cray

c. Darius

d. Woof

12. How many peacekeepers drag Cinna away from Katniss in the glass tube?

a. 3

b. 6

c. 12

d. 1

13. Foxface is a resident of which District?

a. 5

b. 4

c. 6

d. 7

14. Katniss gives a victory speech to residents of which district in Catching Fire?

a. 14

b. 11

c. 12

d. 18

15. What is the lower age limit for participation in the Hunger Games?

a. 16

b. 14

c. 12

d. 18

16. Which of these soundtrack songs has not been released as a stand alone single?

a. Elastic Heart

b. Atlas

c. We Remain

d. Lean

17. Who owned a goat named lady?

a. Katniss

b. Haymitch

c. Peeta

d. Primrose

18. Who locks Crane in a room with Nightlock in The Hunger Games?

a. Haymitch

b. Cato

c. Peeta

d. Snow

19. Which role is played by Bobby Jordan?

a. Chuff

b. Cecelia

c. Seeder

d. Blight

20. What is the name of the event of 75th Hunger Games?

a. Quells Quarter

b. Quarter Question

c. Quarter Quell

d. Question of Quarter

Round 2

1. What is the primary industry of District 10?

a. Textiles

b. Grain

c. Livestock

d. Lumber

2. How many years in the future is the epilogue of "Mockingjay" set?

a. 20

b. 40

c. 50

d. 100

3. Which of these is the name of one of Katniss' prep team?

a. Menia

b. Benia

c. Cenia

d. Venia

4. Johanna Mason comes from which District?

a. 7

b. 4

c. 12

d. 13

5. Patrick St Esprit plays which role in Catching Fire?

a. Woof

b. Romulus Thread

c. Blight

d. Cecelia

6. Who is the director of Catching Fire?

a. Mark Lawrence

b. Frank Lee

c. Fred Leeson

d. Francis Lawrence

7. Which district is the "Fishing District"?

a. 5

b. 1

c. 4

d. 7

8. Which character gives Wiress the nickname "Nuts"?

a. Cray

b. Darius

c. Johanna

d. Gale

9. Who designed the covert art for the Mockingjay novel?

a. Peter) Brien

b. Mark O Brien

c. Henry O Brien

d. Tim O Brien

10. Darius comes from which District in Catching Fire?

a. 12

b. 10

c. 8

d. 4

11. Which Catching Fire actress played Magda in Sex and the City?

a. Jennifer Lawrence

b. Jena Malone

c. Lynn Cohen

d. Elizabeth Banks

12. Peacekeeper Uniforms are made in which industry?

a. 5

b. 8

c. 1

d. 10

13. Who does Katniss say looks like "the colour has all been washed away"?

a. Peeta

b. President Snow

c. Katniss

d. President Coin

14. What is the surname of Peeta in the movie?

a. Dellark

b. Pellark

c. Mellark

d. Fellark

15. In what year was Catching Fire director Francis Lawrence born?

a. 1970

b. 1960

c. 1980

d. 1990

16. In what year was the first Hunger Games book released?

a. 2008

b. 2006

c. 2007

d. 2009

17. Jacqueline Emerson plays which character in The Hunger Games?

a. Foxface

b. Bunnyface

c. Wolfface

d. Vixenface

18. Catching Fire director Francis Lawrence found fame directing what....?

a. Music Videos

b. TV Comedies

c. Stage Plays

d. Commercials

19. Katniss shoots an apple out of which animal's mouth?

a. Vow

b. Pig

c. Horse

d. Dog

20. Which character has the nickname "Nuts"?

a. Beetee

b. Mags

c. Wiress

d. Cinna

Round 3

1. What is the name of Katniss' younger sister?

a. Thistle

b. Julie

c. Primrose

d. Mary

2. Which actor portrays Peeta Mellark in Catching Fire?

a. Woody Harrelson

b. Liam Hemsworth

c. Josh Hutcherson

d. Stanley Tucci

3. Who is "hijacked" in Mockingjay Part 1?

a. Haymitch

b. Primrose

c. President Coin

d. Peeta

4. What is the first name of Catching Fire actor Mr. Calfin?

a. Steve

b. Sam

c. Simon

d. Sean

5. What is the main industry of District 11?

a. Lumber

b. Textiles

c. Agriculture

d. Transportation

6. The name of Panem translates as what?

a. Wine

b. Bread

c. Beer

d. Toast

7. Lyme hails from which District?

a. 4

b. 2

c. 5

d. 7

8. Complete the tagline from the Catching Fire poster "Remember who the ____ is"?

a. Enemy

b. Friend

c. Capitol

d. Soldier

9. Textiles is the main industry of which District?

a. 5

b. 8

c. 3

d. 1

10. In what year was Hunger Games star Josh Hutcherson born?

a. 1992

b. 1978

c. 1996

d. 1974

11. Which British band contribute the single "Atlas" to the soundtrack?

a. Mumford and Suns

b. Muse

c. Coldplay

d. U2

12. What number is Catching Fire in The Hunger Games series?

a. 3rd

b. 1st

c. 2nd

d. 4th

13. Maria Howell plays which role in Catching Fire?

a. Chuff

b. Seeder

c. Cashmere

d. Brutus

14. Stef Dawson plays which character in Mockingjay Part 1?

a. Susie

b. Annie

c. Julie

d. Mary

15. Which character is played by Amanda Plummer in Catching Fire?

a. Miress

b. Tiress

c. Wiress

d. Liress

16. Who writes a book with Peeta in "Mockingjay"?

a. Annie

b. Primrose

c. Finnick

d. Katniss

17. Blight comes for which District?

a. 7

b. 4

c. 1

d. 11

18. Who plays Haymitch Abernathy in The Hunger Games

a. Lenny Kravitz

b. Liam Hemsworth

c. Josh Hutchersn

d. Woody Harrelson

19. Sarita Choudhury plays which character in Mockingjay Part 1?

a. Megeria

b. Egeria

c. Fegeria

d. Segeria

20. How is Cato killed in The Hunger Games?

a. Wild Beasts

b. Katniss Bow

c. Drowning

d. Fire

Round 4

1. What does Lavinia become?

a. Lavox

b. Avox

c. Savox

d. Davox

2. Which character in the film has the nickname Volts?

a. Cray

b. Haymitch

c. Beetee

d. Woof

3. How old is Peeta Mellark in Catching Fire?

a. 16

b. 18

c. 21

d. 10

4. Who did Thread replace as Peacekeeper?

a. President Snow

b. Gale

c. Woof

d. Cray

5. What position did Seneca Crane once hold?

a. Referee

b. Head Position

c. Head Gamekeeper

d. Judge

6. What is the first of Effie Trinket actress Ms. Banks?

a. Jennifer

b. Edna

c. Elizabeth

d. Jessica

7. During which film is Katniss filmed signing "The Hanging Tree"?

a. Mockingjay Part 1

b. Mockingjay Part 2

c. Catching Fire

d. The Hunger Games

8. Taylor St Clair plays a character named what in Catching Fire?

a. Gripper

b. Ripper

c. Lipper

d. Flipper

9. What much did the first Hunger Games movie take at the Box Office?

a. $33 million

b. $2 billion

c. $700 million

d. $178 million

10. Who does Katniss spot hiding in a tree in The Hunger Games opening battles?

a. Fue

b. Sue

c. Lue

d. Rue

11. For what crime is Gale whipped by Thread?

a. Turkey Poaching

b. Vegetable Theft

c. Horse Theft

d. Fishing

12. Who kills Glimmer?

a. Romulous

b. Snow

c. Primose

d. Katniss

13. Who does Katniss encounter in the final of Mockingjay?

a. Peeta

b. Primrose

c. Everdeen

d. President Snow

14. What is Plutrach's surname?

a. Nightsbee

b. Heavensbee

c. Timesbee

d. Hellsbee

15. Haymitch Abernathy suffers from withdrawal of what in Catching Fire?

a. Alcohol

b. Drugs

c. Smoking

d. Tea

16. Nina Jacobson has what role in Catching Fire?

a. Composer

b. Producer

c. Director

d. Screenwriter

17. What is Foxfaces real name?

a. Imran

b. Julie

c. Armadno

d. Its Unknown

18. "She's not who they think she is. She just wants to save her skin." Which character speaks this line in Catching Fire?

a. President Snow

b. Katniss

c. Plutrach

d. Gale

19. What is the first name of Ms Shields, an actress in Catching Fire?

a. Tree

b. Willow

c. Bark

d. Wood

20. What role does Caesar Flickerman have in Catching Fire?

a. Bookmaker

b. Referee

c. Announcer

d. Soldier

Round 5

1. What is the name of the character played by Jack Quaid?

a. Larvel

b. Travel

c. Marvel

d. Parvel

2. What is Effie's surname?

a. Drinket

b. Trinket

c. Linket

d. Sinket

3. Which District's industry is Power?

a. 6

b. 4

c. 5

d. 7

4. Romulus Thread was the overseer for the Burning of the….?

a. Cob

b. Hob

c. Dob

d. Bob

5. Wiress is given what nickname by Johanna?

a. Screws

b. Bolts

c. Volts

d. Nuts

6. Titus hails from which District?

a. 4

b. 6

c. 3

d. 1

7. Stef Dawson plays which role in Catching Fire?

a. Maria

b. Annie

c. Gloss

d. Brutus

8. Who is appointed as Katniss' stylist in mockingjay?

a. Beffie

b. Seffie

c. Leffie

d. Effie

9. Which one of the following is the correct name for a screenwriter for Catching Fire?

a. Francis Beaufoy

b. Steven Beaufoy

c. Michael Beaufoy

d. Simon Beaufoy

10. How old is President Coin?

a. 50

b. 40

c. 30

d. 60

11. What nationality is Catching Fire star Liam Hemsworth?

a. English

b. American

c. Australian

d. Canadian

12. Who agrees to be the "mockingjay"?

a. President Snow

b. Peeta

c. Prim

d. Katniss

13. John Castino plays which role in Catching Fire?

a. Woof

b. Blight

c. Cecelia

d. Seeder

14. Which district is located where Florida is today?

a. 7

b. 5

c. 11

d. 9

15. Marvel comes from which district?

a. 6

b. 1

c. 8

d. 10

16. When was MockingJay Part 1 released in cinemas?

a. 2010

b. 2012

c. 2014

d. 2008

17. Which District is known for masonry?

a. 4

b. 3

c. 2

d. 5

18. The quote "ladies first" is most associated with which character?

a. Haymitch

b. Effie

c. Peeta

d. Katniss

19. What colour eyes are we told Prim has?

a. Red

b. Blue

c. Green

d. Brown

20. The Dark Days occurred how many years before The Hunger Games is set?

a. 199

b. 75

c. 289

d. 1089

Round 6

1. What is the name of district 11's male tribune in The Hunger Games?

a. Dove

b. Love

c. Clove

d. Stove

2. What is the name of the rebel leader in District 13 in Mockingjay?

a. President Rome

b. President Coin

c. President Money

d. President Paper

3. A boy from which district is the first person killed in the Hunger Games novels?

a. 9

b. 1

c. 13

d. 4

4. Katniss kills whom with a bow to end their suffering of being attacked by beasts?

a. Peeta

b. Cato

c. Rue

d. Snow

5. Annie Cresta is the lover of which character?

a. Finnick

b. Katniss

c. Peeta

d. Prim

6. Octavia is a member of which characters prep team?

a. Haymitch

b. Katniss

c. Peeta

d. Effie

7. Which Patti Smith song features on the soundtrack of Catching Fire?

a. Capital Day

b. Capital Deeds

c. Capital Hill

d. Capital Letter

8. What is Primrose's main skill which she inherited from her mother?

a. Medium

b. Healer

c. Soldier

d. Miner

9. Who plays Claudius Templesmith in Catching Fire?

a. Woody Harrelson

b. Donald Sutherland

c. Stanley Tucci

d. Toby Jones

10. Who directed Mocking Jay part 1?

a. William Jenkins

b. Damien Sanding

c. Frank Turner

d. Francis Lawrence

11. Everybody Wants to Rule The World is a soundtrack song by which band in Catching Fire?

a. Lorde

b. The Lumineers

c. The National

d. Coldplay

12. Jennifer Lawrence suffered an accident in filming Catching Fire that left her deaf for how many days?

a. 6

b. 4

c. 7

d. 9

13. What is the occupation of Peeta's father?

a. Miner

b. Butcher

c. Baker

d. Soldier

14. What is the upper age limit for participation in the Hunger Games?

a. 38

b. 28

c. 18

d. 48

15. In Mockingjay, who devises a controversial strategy to win District 2?

a. Gale

b. Katniss

c. Snow

d. Haymitch

16. Philip Seymour Hoffman plays which character in Mockingjay?

a. Beetee

b. Plutarch

c. Cressida

d. Boggs

17. What is the only day on which Gale can hunt?

a. Saturday

b. Monday

c. Sunday

d. Friday

18. Who submitted three songs for the soundtrack which were all turned down?

a. Bruno Mars

b. James Blunt

c. Justin Timberlake

d. Ed Sheeran

19. Who sends White Roses to District 13 in Mockingjay to tease Katniss?

a. Haymitch

b. President Coin

c. Cesar Flickerman

d. President Snow

20. Katniss changes her mind after she notices which character is being used to quell rebellion?

a. Peeta

b. Her Mother

c. Primrose

d. Haymitch

Round 7

1. Jeffrey Wright plays which character in Catching Fire?

a. Beetee

b. Teebee

c. Peetee

d. Teepee

2. Who does Katniss try to convince to eat dealing nightlock at the end of The Hunger Games?

a. Thresh

b. Rue

c. Primrose Everdeen

d. Peeta

3. Complete the final sombre quote from the books "There are much worse games to ___"?

a. Play

b. Win

c. Loose

d. Arrive

4. Katniss table manners upset whom?

a. Haymitch

b. Effie

c. Peeta

d. Snow

5. What title does Mr. Thread have in the film?

a. Knight

b. Lord

c. Commander

d. Judge

6. What is Haymitch's role in The Hunger Games?

a. Referee

b. Trainer

c. Commentator

d. Doctor

7. What hashtag could fans use to access exclusive shots from the movie in the months prior to release?

a. #explorehungergames

b. #Hungergamesexplorer

c. #HGE

d. #Hungergamesnews

8. Who does Mags volunteer to replace in the games?

a. Katniss

b. Primrose

c. Gale

d. Annie

9. Josh Hutcherson plays which character in the Hunger Games movies?

a. Peeta Mellark

b. Gale

c. Haymitch

d. Primrose Everdeen

10. Which District is home of Beetee?

a. 12

b. 4

c. 3

d. 10

11. "I can't go on acting for the cameras and then just ignoring each other in real life." is spoken by which character in Catching Fire?

a. Peeta

b. Katniss

c. Haymitch

d. Gale

12. When was Hunger Games author Suzanne Collins born?

a. 1982

b. 1972

c. 1962

d. 1942

13. What nationality is Catching Fire Author Suzanne Collins?

a. Canadian

b. English

c. American

d. French

14. Who suggest to Crane that there should be a rule to allow 2 winners?

a. Snow

b. Katniss

c. Rue

d. Haymitch

15. Claudius Templesmith has what role in Catching Fire?

a. Announcer

b. Referee

c. Bookmaker

d. Soldier

16. What is the title of The Hungers Games soundtrack?

a. From District 10 and Here

b. From District 11 and Outside

c. From District 12 and Beyond

d. From District 4 and More

17. Supply of what runs out in District 12 in Catching Fire?

a. Coal

b. Alcohol

c. Water

d. Food

18. Effie Trinket is the escort for the tributes of what district in Catching Fire?

a. 12

b. 4

c. 7

d. 9

19. Who express his love for Katniss in television interviews in the first movie?

a. Snow

b. Haymitch

c. Gale

d. Peeta

20. Which singer performs "Mirror" on the soundtrack of Catching Fire?

a. Patti Smith

b. Emile Sande

c. Christina Aguilera

d. Ellie Goulding

Round 8

1. In what year was Hunger Games star Liam Hemsworth born?

a. 1990

b. 1985

c. 1980

d. 1975

2. Which district is located South of the Lake formerly known as Ontario?

a. 4

b. 1

c. 8

d. 6

3. Who is the music supervisor on Catching Fire?

a. Derek Strong

b. Peter Jones

c. Mark Lubjuana

d. Alexandra Pastavas

4. In which part of Panem is District 4 located?

a. West

b. North

c. East

d. South

5. Seeder is a Hunger Games victor from which District?

a. 3

b. 11

c. 5

d. 8

6. Catching Fire actress Elizabeth Banks was born in which year?

a. 1974

b. 1988

c. 1965

d. 1982

7. How does Effie transport the tributes to the Capitol?

a. Train

b. Plane

c. Hovercraft

d. Orbs

8. Who composed the music for the Hunger Games?

a. Marc Clotet

b. John Smith

c. Eddie Jenkins

d. James Newton Howard

9. Haymitch struggles with an addiction to what?

a. Alcohol

b. Drugs

c. Violence

d. TV

10. What weapon does Clove use when Katniss is nearly killed?

a. Gun

b. Bow

c. Knife

d. Bomb

11. Who is captured at the end of Catching Fire by the Capitol?

a. Primrose

b. Peeta

c. Katniss

d. Johanna

12. Who does Snow lock in a room with Nightlock in the Hunger Games?

a. Primrose Everdeen

b. Peeta

c. Katniss

d. Crane

13. What does Katniss fight for with a man from District 9 as the Hunger Games begin?

a. Wine

b. Backpack

c. Weapon

d. Food

14. What district do Katniss Everdeen and her family hail from?

a. 4

b. 12

c. 14

d. 7

15. Who is appointed to be Katniss bodyguard in Mockingjay?

a. Fale

b. Dale

c. Male

d. Gale

16. Who kills Wiress?

a. Gale

b. Darius

c. Cray

d. Gloss

17. When was the first Hunger Games movie released?

a. 2010

b. 2014

c. 2012

d. 2008

18. How many entrants are invited to take part in the 75th Hunger Games?

a. 24

b. 12

c. 8

d. 16

19. Which district is dominated by Farmland?

a. 1

b. 12

c. 9

d. 4

20. "People are looking to you, Katniss. You've given them an opportunity. " is a line spoken by which character in Catching Fire?

a. Gale

b. President Snow

c. Haymitch

d. Annie

Round 9

1. Which actor plays Marvel?

a. Wes Bentley

b. Dayo Okeniyi

c. Jack Quaid

d. Alexander Ludwig

2. Which character is nicknamed Nuts?

a. Primrose

b. Mags

c. Wiress

d. Katniss

3. Transportation is the main industry of which district?

a. 4

b. 6

c. 7

d. 9

4. How many winners does Haymitch suggest there should be in The Hunger Games?

a. 1

b. 3

c. 5

d. 6

5. What natural disaster broke the dam which led to Annie Crests victory in The Hunger Games?

a. Tsunami

b. Volcanoe

c. Earthquake

d. Tornado

6. What edition of the Hunger Games takes place in Catching fire?

a. 77th

b. 75th

c. 80th

d. 74th

7. Complete the title of a song from the Catching Fire soundtrack "Shooting Arrows at the…"?

a. Sky

b. Moon

c. Stars

d. Enemy

8. Which District is known for luxury items?

a. 10

b. 5

c. Rocky Mountains

d. 12

9. Who is being tortured in the Capitol in "Mockingjay"?

a. Finnick

b. Annie

c. Katniss

d. Peeta

10. Which character is resuscitated by Finnick?

a. Primrose

b. Katniss

c. Peeta

d. Gale

11. What will "Tomorrow Be ___" according the title of the song on the Hunger Games soundtrack?

a. Colder

b. Warmer

c. Kinder

d. Never

12. Which Cast member is the brother in law of Emily Blunt?

a. Lenny Kravitz

b. Woody Harrelson

c. Stanley Tucci

d. Josh Hutcherson

13. Who whips Gale for poaching a turkey?

a. Octavia

b. Cray

c. Snow

d. Thread

14. President Snow is what age?

a. 56

b. 76

c. 36

d. 106

15. What part of an Avox is removed?

a. Nose

b. Ears

c. Tounge

d. Hands

16. Who has 2 children with Peeta?

a. Annie

b. Primrose

c. Finnick

d. Katniss

17. The people of which district riot when Rue is killed in The Hunger Games?

a. 16

b. 11

c. 2

d. 7

18. Cashmere is from which District?

a. 1

b. 4

c. 6

d. 8

19. Who does Katniss begin to think its trying to take power in "Mockingjay"?

a. Haymitch

b. Peeta

c. Gale

d. Coin

20. Who contributes the song "Eyes Open" to the Hunger Games soundtrack?

a. Paramore

b. Lady Gaga

c. Lilly Allen

d. Taylor Swift

Round 10

1. What is Katniss' surname?

a. Evergreen

b. Everdeen

c. Everseen

d. Everbeen

2. Which award winning screen writer wrote Mockingjay's screenplay?

a. Danny Bleak

b. Danny Weak

c. Danny Strong

d. Danny Dark

3. What does Katniss ensure Primrose is allowed to keep in her negotiations to join the Rebellion?

a. Name

b. Cat

c. Hair

d. Clothes

4. Who does Cesar Flickerman interview in Mocking jay Part 1?

a. Primrose

b. Katniss

c. Coin

d. Peeta

5. District 1 is located in which direction from the Capitol?

a. North

b. East

c. South

d. West

6. Which district does Rue hail from?

a. 16

b. 14

c. 11

d. 7

7. Who hijacks the news feeds to broadcast Katniss rage in Mockingjay?

a. Leetee

b. Weepee

c. Seetee

d. Beetee

8. What relationship does Katniss pretend to have with Gale?

a. Father

b. Brother

c. Cousin

d. Son

9. What song is Katniss filmed singing in Mockingjay?

a. The Hanging Rod

b. The Hanging Brach

c. The Hanging Tree

d. The Hanging Plant

10. We are told that Prim has what colour hair?

a. Red

b. Blonde

c. Black

d. Brown

11. Which character is famous for her green suits?

a. Peeta

b. Haymitch

c. Effie

d. Katniss

12. From which District does Enobaria hail from?

a. 2

b. 5

c. 12

d. 10

13. Who composed the music for Catching Fire?

a. James Howard Newton

b. Newton James Howard

c. Howard Newton James

d. James Newton Howard

14. What is the name of the individual who interviews Peeta in Mockingjay Part 1?

a. Marvin Emnes

b. Dwayne Eddy

c. Cesar Flickerman

d. Julio Rodriguez

15. What is Madge's surname?

a. Oversee

b. Undersee

c. Longsee

d. Shortsee

16. From which District are the runaways Katniss encounters in Catching Fire?

a. 8

b. 5

c. 4

d. 11

17. Who plays Caesar Flickerman in the movie?

a. Josh Hutcherson

b. Woody Harrelson

c. Lenny Kravitz

d. Stanley Tucci

18. What colour is Caser Flickermans hair and eyes?

a. White

b. Black

c. Blue

d. Brown

19. What colour hair does Primrose Everdeen have?

a. Brown

b. Blonde

c. Black

d. Ginger

20. Who plays Effie Trinket in Catching Fire?

a. Willow Shields

b. Jennifer Lawrence

c. Sam Claffin

d. Elizabeth Banks

Round 11

1. Rue dies in which of the Hunger Games movies?

a. Mocking Jay Part 1

b. The Hunger Games

c. Mocking Jay Part 2

d. Catching Fire

2. Peetas father has what occupation?

a. Butcher

b. Baker

c. Winemaker

d. Brewer

3. Which of these figures wrote the screenplay for Mocking Jay?

a. Danny Smith

b. Danny Tough

c. Danny Evans

d. Danny Strong

4. Who utters the line "Tonight, Turn your weapons to the Capitol"?

a. Effie

b. Haymitch

c. Peeta

d. Katniss

5. Who gives CPR to Peeta to revive him?

a. Gale

b. Katniss

c. Primrose

d. Finnick

6. Prim is killed in what novel?

a. The Hunger Games

b. Mockingjay

c. Catching Fire

d. None

7. Which role does Bruno Gunn play?

a. Gloss

b. Wiress

c. Mags

d. Brutus

8. How old is Primrose Everdeen in Catching Fire?

a. 13

b. 11

c. 15

d. 17

9. Cinna nicknames Katniss "The Girl on…"?

a. Fire

b. A high

c. Love

d. Heaven

10. What is the title of the sequel to Catching Fire in the Hunger Games series?

a. Mockingray

b. Mockingday

c. Mockingjay

d. Mockinglay

11. Firearms are produced in which District?

a. 3

b. 6

c. 1

d. 9

12. Who trains Katniss for the first Hunger Games?

a. President Snow

b. Gale

c. Primrose Everdeen

d. Haymitch

13. Katniss travels to whose mansion in Mockingjay?

a. Coin

b. Snow

c. Annie

d. Peeta

14. "Remember who the real enemy is". Which character speaks this line in Catching Fire?

a. Haymitch

b. Katniss

c. Primrose Everdeen

d. Gale

15. What does Katniss shoot from the mouth of a pig?

a. Peach

b. Apple

c. Plum

d. Pear

16. Which district does Gale Hawthorne come form?

a. 10

b. 11

c. 12

d. 6

17. What Budget did Catching Fire have?

a. $40 Million

b. $140 Million

c. $240 Million

d. $340 Million

18. Which edition of the Hunger Games was won by Annie Cresta?

a. 90th

b. 80th

c. 100th

d. 70th

19. Catching Fire actress Jennifer Lawrence was born in which year?

a. 1990

b. 1988

c. 1986

d. 1984

20. What is Gale's surname?

a. Tribes

b. Hawtorne

c. Miles

d. Endo

Round 12

1. What is the name of President Coins rebellious strategy?

a. Trust and Hope

b. Souls and love

c. Hearts and Minds

d. Days and Nights

2. Which district has Graphite as its main industry?

a. 7

b. 12

c. 5

d. 13

3. What weapon is Finnick Odair most associated with?

a. Gun

b. Knife

c. Trident

d. Bow

4. How many novels are there in the Hunger Games series?

a. 3

b. 4

c. 5

d. 6

5. How old is Gale Hawthorne in Catching Fire?

a. 19

b. 12

c. 15

d. 22

6. What is name of Finnick Odairs mentor who appears in the movie?

a. Bags

b. Mags

c. Dags

d. Clags

7. What is the main industry of District 8?

a. Transportation

b. Lumber

c. Textiles

d. Fishing

8. In what year was the Catching Fire novel released?

a. 2009

b. 2010

c. 2008

d. 2007

9. In which year was Catching Fire actor Toby Jones born?

a. 1966

b. 1977

c. 1988

d. 1955

10. "You understand, that what ever I do, it comes back to you and mom." is a line from which character in Catching Fire?

a. Katniss

b. President Snow

c. Primrose Everdeen

d. Gale

11. Who plays Katniss Everdeen in the movies?

a. Jennifer Grey

b. Jennifer Aniston

c. Jennifer Hudson

d. Jennifer Lawrence

12. Who is co-winner of the 74th Hunger Games with Katniss?

a. Thresh

b. Rue

c. Primrose Everdeen

d. Peeta

13. Leven Rambin plays which character?

a. Cato

b. Glimmer

c. Clove

d. Katniss

14. Which of the following is the only living victor in District 12 at the start of the film?

a. Cinna

b. Cray

c. Woof

d. Haymitch

15. Complete the title of the Maroon 5 track on the Hunger Games soundtrack "Come Away to the ___"?

a. Water

b. Fire

c. Love

d. Trust

16. Who won the 50th Hunger Games?

a. Primrose

b. Katniss

c. Peeta

d. Haymitch

17. Which character is played by Bruce Bundy?

a. Flavius

b. Cinna

c. Octavia

d. Ripper

18. In which district are a team of peacekeepers killed by land mines in Mockingkay?

a. 7

b. 3

c. 5

d. 11

19. What is the first name of President Coin?

a. Malma

b. Alma

c. Salma

d. Falma

20. Robert Knepper plays which character in Mockingjay Part 1?

a. Pious

b. Antonius

c. Julius

d. Brutus

Round 13

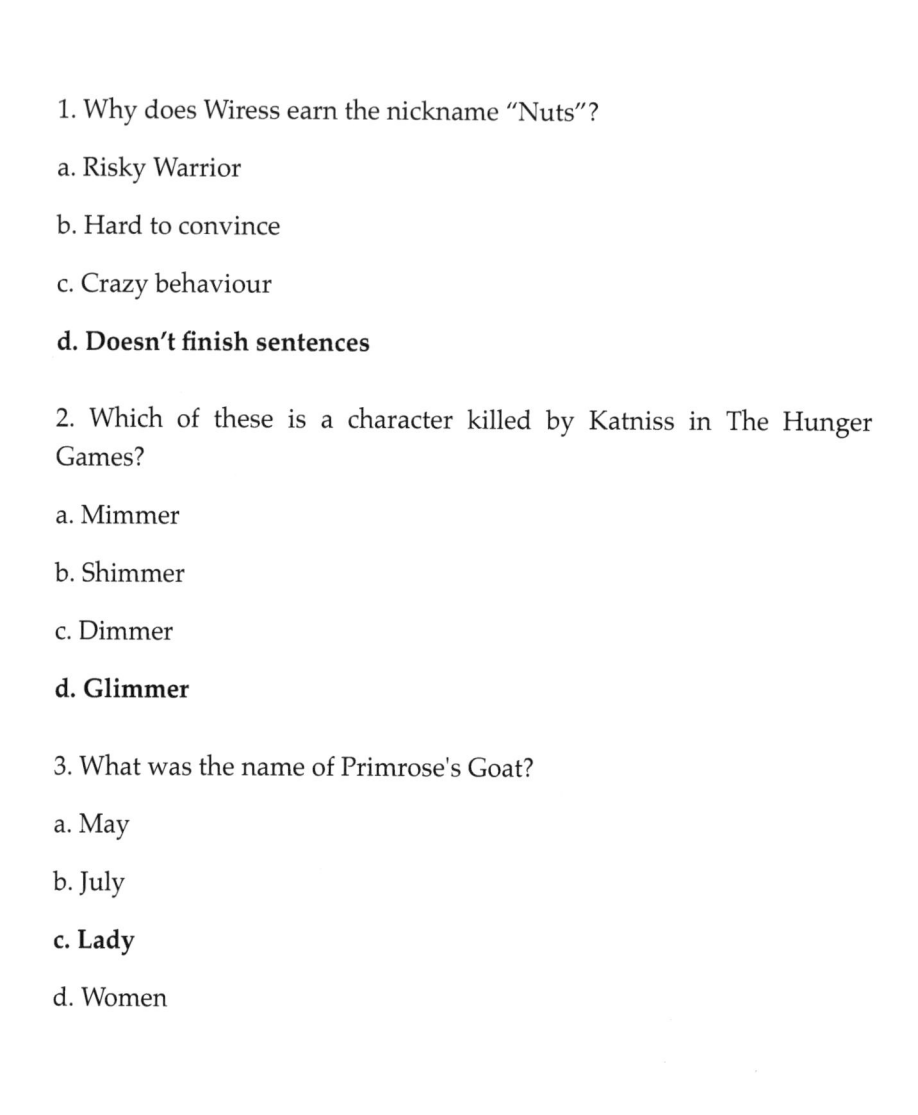

1. Why does Wiress earn the nickname "Nuts"?

a. Risky Warrior

b. Hard to convince

c. Crazy behaviour

d. Doesn't finish sentences

2. Which of these is a character killed by Katniss in The Hunger Games?

a. Mimmer

b. Shimmer

c. Dimmer

d. Glimmer

3. What was the name of Primrose's Goat?

a. May

b. July

c. Lady

d. Women

4. Elden Henson plays which character in Mockingjay Part 1?

a. Pollux

b. Mollux

c. Sollux

d. Dollux

5. What is the name of Taylor Swift's song on the Hunger Games Soundtrack?

a. Eyes Awake

b. Eyes Shut

c. Eyes Open

d. Eyes Wide

6. During which event was the first teaser trailer for Catching Fire premiered?

a. MTV Awards

b. Superbowl

c. Wrestlemania

d. World Series

7. Who is the author of The Hunger Games?

a. Stephen King

b. JK Rowling

c. George RR Martin

d. Suzanne Collins

8. Residents of District 2 are known as "___ of the Capitol"?

a. Demons

b. Pets

c. Friends

d. Enemies

9. How many children do Katniss and Peeta have?

a. 2

b. 3

c. 4

d. 5

10. Finnick Odair is portrayed by which actor in Catching Fire?

a. Sam Claflin

b. Toby Jones

c. Donald Sutherland

d. Stanley Tucci

11. Natalie Dormer plays which character in Mockingjay Part 1?

a. Lessida

b. Cressida

c. Sessida

d. Fessida

12. What is the relationship between Katniss and Primrose?

a. Mother/Daughter

b. Cousins

c. Sisters

d. Auntie/Neice

13. "Would you like to be in a real war? Imagine thousands of your people, dead. Your loved ones, gone." is a line spoken by which character in Catching Fire?

a. President Snow

b. Katniss

c. Haymitch

d. Gale

14. What is the main industry of District 9?

a. Lumber

b. Textiles

c. Grain

d. Transportation

15. Who announced on Twitter that her song "We Remain" will feature on the Catching Fire Soundtrack?

a. Lady Gaga

b. Britney Spears

c. Madonna

d. Christina Aguilera

16. Who notices the soft spot in the force field surrounding the Capitol?

a. Woof

b. Haymitch

c. Cray

d. Beetee

17. What is the name of the Coldplay song on the soundtrack of Catching Fire?

a. World

b. Globe

c. Atlas

d. Planets

18. E Roger Mitchell plays which role in Catching Fire?

a. Chuff

b. Cashmere

c. Brutus

d. Wiress

19. Rue is from which District?

a. 3

b. 11

c. 5

d. 8

20. What does President Snow send to District 13 in Mockingjay Part 1 to tease Katniss?

a. Lillies

b. White Roses

c. Sunflowers

d. Orchids

Round 14

1. Which Districts inhabits are known as the "Pets" of the Capitol?

a. 6

b. 5

c. 2

d. 8

2. Who killed Seneca Crane?

a. Woof

b. Cray

c. Gale

d. President Snow

3. When was the novel of Mockingjay released?

a. 2002

b. 2006

c. 2010

d. 1998

4. The Capitol has a non aggression pact with which District?

a. District 10

b. District 13

c. District 9

d. District 1

5. What character does Donald Sutherland play in Catching Fire?

a. Cinna

b. President Snow

c. Caesar Flickerman

d. Haymitch Abernathy

6. District 7's main industry is what?

a. Lumber

b. Transportation

c. Fishing

d. Mining

7. Katniss is enraged by a brutal massacre in which venue in District 8 during Mockingjay part 1?

a. Shop

b. Hospital

c. Mall

d. School

8. What weapon does Foxface use?

a. Gun

b. Bow

c. Knife

d. Bomb

9. Who kills Rue?

a. Primrose Everdeen

b. Snow

c. Cato

d. Marvel

10. What is Effie's surname in Catching Fire?

a. Drinket

b. Trinket

c. Brinket

d. Linket

11. Gale Song features on the soundtrack of Catching Fire. Which band perform this?

a. The Lumineers

b. The National

c. Coldplay

d. Imagine Dragons

12. District 4, featured in the movie, is most associated with what industry in Catching Fire?

a. Fishing

b. Baking

c. Mining

d. Gold

13. Who plays Katniss Everdeen in Catching Fire?

a. Sam Claffin

b. Elizabeth Banks

c. Willow Shields

d. Jennifer Lawrence

14. Who is the only escort to survive the rebellion?

a. Katniss

b. Haymitch

c. Peeta

d. Effie

15. What is the name of the lottery to determine who plays in the Hunger Games?

a. The Deeping

b. The Seaping

c. The Reaping

d. The Damning

16. Cato comes from which district?

a. 2

b. 5

c. 7

d. 12

17. What does Katniss convince Peeta to at with her in The Hunger Games?

a. Daylock

b. Nightlock

c. Sunlock

d. Glowlock

18. How are a team of peacekeepers killed in district 7 during Mockingjay?

a. Land Mines

b. Electric Chair

c. Beheading

d. Shot

19. Cato is played by which actor in The Hunger Games?

a. Alexander Ludwig

b. Jack Quaid

c. Dayo Okeniyi

d. Wes Bentley

20. What is the name of the leader of district 13's film team?

a. Messida

b. Lessida

c. Cressida

d. Fessida

Round 15

1. Who is killed by bombs whilst trying to save children in "Mockingjay"?

a. President Snow

b. Everdeen

c. Peeta

d. Primrose

2. Where is the hospital, seen of a brutal massacre in Mockingjay?

a. District 11

b. District 5

c. District 8

d. District 1

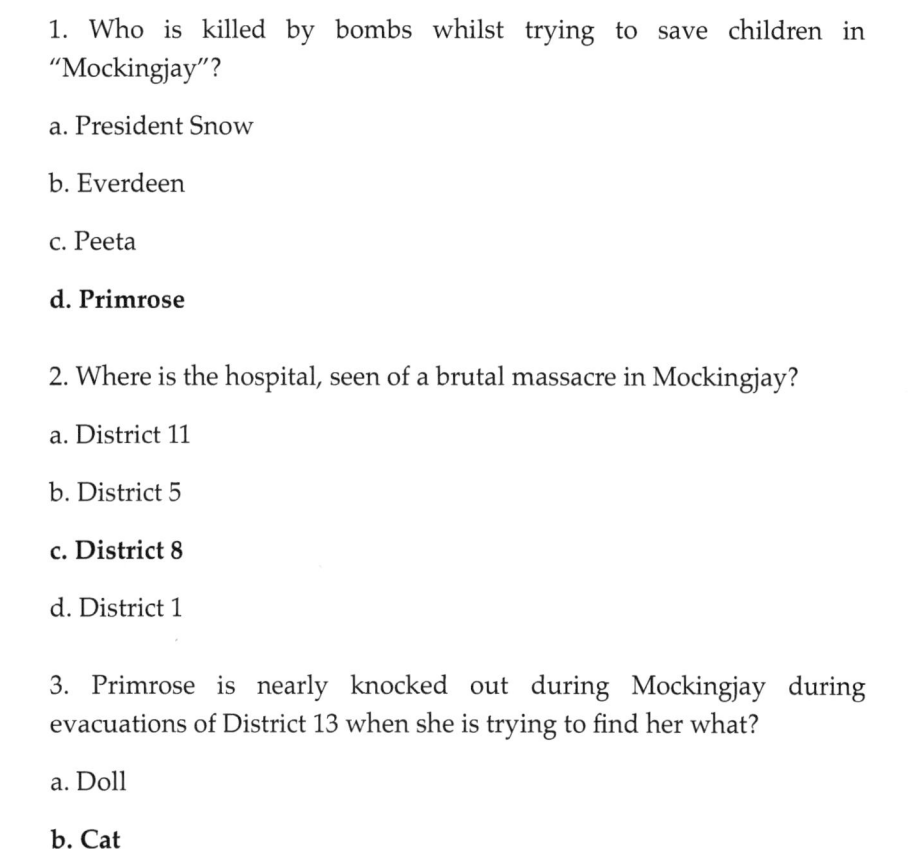

3. Primrose is nearly knocked out during Mockingjay during evacuations of District 13 when she is trying to find her what?

a. Doll

b. Cat

c. Purse

d. Sister

4. Katniss hails from which district?

a. 10

b. 12

c. 8

d. 5

5. What is the population of Panem?

a. 44 million

b. 10000

c. 4.5 million

d. 2 billion

6. What role does Alan Ritchson play?

a. Wiress

b. Brutus

c. Gloss

d. Mags

7. Johanne Mason hails from which District?

a. 7

b. 4

c. 8

d. 11

8. Caesar Flickerman lives where?

a. Capitol

b. District 1

c. District 2

d. District 12

9. Which film company produces The Hunger Games movies?

a. Universal

b. United Artists

c. Seagram

d. Lionsgate

10. Enobaria ripped what part of an opponents body off with her teeth in Catching Fire?

a. Throat

b. Ears

c. Nose

d. Fingers

11. Who plays Seneca Crane in The Hunger Games?

a. Dayo Okeniyi

b. Alexander Ludwig

c. Jack Quaid

d. Wes Bentley

12. Livestock is the main industry of which District?

a. 12

b. 10

c. 7

d. 3

13. What age was Gale Hawthorne when he met Katniss Everdeen?

a. 16

b. 14

c. 21

d. 5

14. What is Seneca's surname?

a. Drane

b. Crane

c. Brane

d. Mane

15. How did Jennifer Lawrence lose her hearing during filming of Catching Fire?

a. Dived into a pool

b. Hit with Boom

c. Explosion in scene

d. Hit with an arrow

16. In which city did Catching Fire have its World Premiere?

a. London

b. Paris

c. New York

d. Sydney

17. Amanda Stenberg plays which character in the first movie?

a. Rue

b. Clove

c. Thresh

d. Glimmer

18. What is the industry of District 13?

a. Grain

b. Livestock

c. Graphite

d. Textiles

19. Who says "Happy Hunger Games! And may the odds be in your favour"?

a. Katniss

b. Haymitch

c. Peeta

d. Effie

20. "You saved my life. You gave me a chance." is a line spoken by which character in Catching Fire?

a. Primrose Everdeen

b. President Snow

c. Annie

d. Gale

Round 16

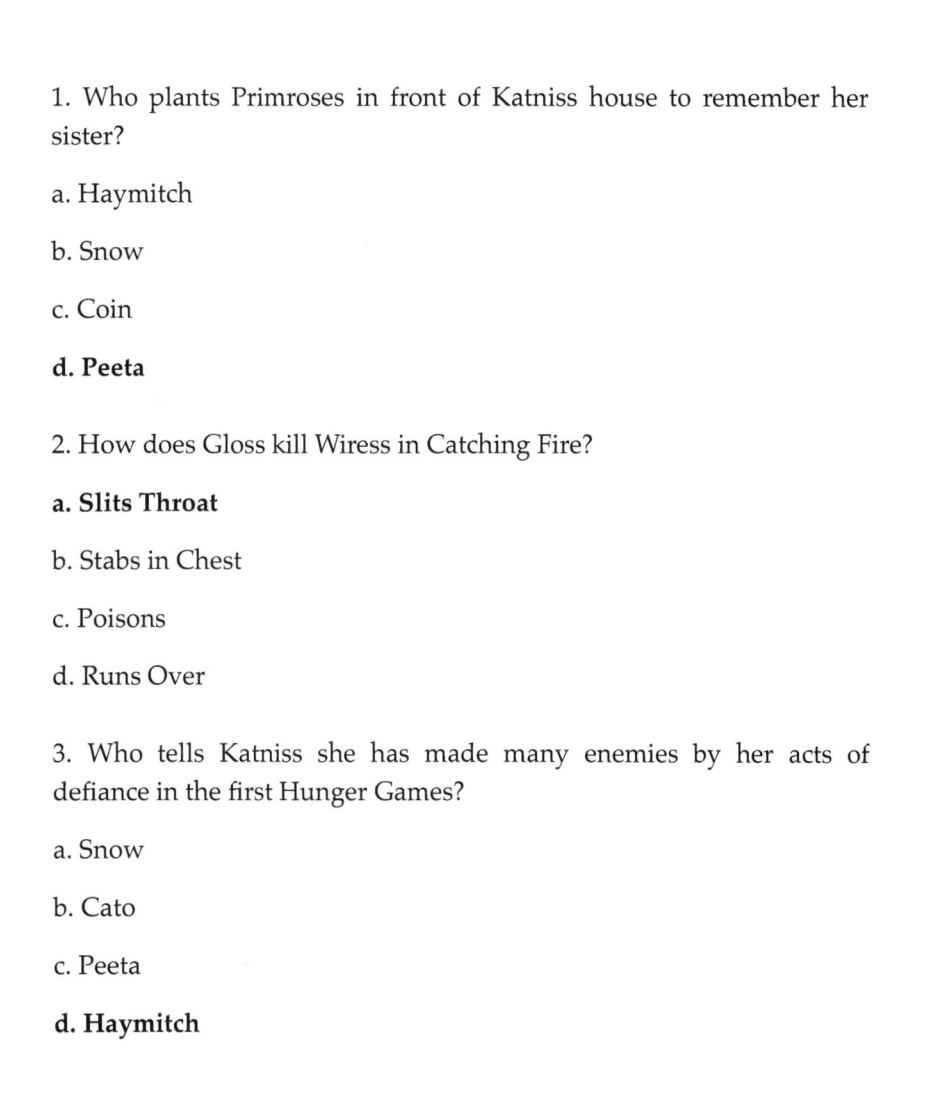

1. Who plants Primroses in front of Katniss house to remember her sister?

a. Haymitch

b. Snow

c. Coin

d. Peeta

2. How does Gloss kill Wiress in Catching Fire?

a. Slits Throat

b. Stabs in Chest

c. Poisons

d. Runs Over

3. Who tells Katniss she has made many enemies by her acts of defiance in the first Hunger Games?

a. Snow

b. Cato

c. Peeta

d. Haymitch

4. Katniss leaves whose side in The Hunger Games to get medicine?

a. Primrose

b. Peeta

c. Clove

d. Thresh

5. Where does "the boy with the bad leg" hail from?

a. District 13

b. District 9

c. District 10

d. District 3

6. Who plays Gale Hawthorne in the film?

a. Josh Hutcherson

b. Woody Harrelson

c. Stanley Tucci

d. Liam Hemsworth

7. Trains are made in which District?

a. 4

b. 2

c. 6

d. 8

8. Nelson Ascencio plays which role in Catching Fire?

a. Ripper

b. Flavius

c. Octavia

d. Cinna

9. Who escorts Katniss and Peeta to the Capitol in the first movie?

a. Leffie

b. Meffie

c. Seffie

d. Effie

10. Paula Malconson plays the mother of which character?

a. Primrose

b. Katniss

c. Gale

d. President Snow

11. What role is played by Elena Sanchez?

a. Chuff

b. Seeder

c. Cecelia

d. Cashmere

12. Which of these series of books is also by Catching Fire author Suzanne Collins?

a. The Undergound Chronicles

b. The Overland Chronicles

c. The Overload Chronicles

d. The Underland Chronicles

13. What is Darius turned into?

a. A Goat

b. An Avox

c. A Spock

d. A Doddle

14. What is the middle name of author Suzanne Collins?

a. Edith

b. Julie

c. Marie

d. Natty

15. Wiress comes from which District?

a. 8

b. 1

c. 6

d. 3

16. What is the surname of the character played by Jennifer Lawrence in Catching Fire?

a. Evergreen

b. Everbeen

c. Everdeen

d. Everseen

17. Who plays Thresh in the movies?

a. Jack Quaid

b. Wes Bentley

c. Alexander Ludwig

d. Dayo Okeniyi

18. Who unleashes the wild beasts that kill Thresh?

a. Primrose Everdeen

b. Snow

c. Katniss

d. Crane

19. What was the name of Prim's cat?

a. Mary

b. Baby

c. Buttercup

d. Sue

20. Sia Furler contributes what song to the soundtrack of Catching Fire?

a. Plastic Heart

b. Elastic Heart

c. Broken Heart

d. Glass Heart

Round 17

1. Who says "I Volunteer as your tribute"?

a. Effie

b. Haymitch

c. Peeta

d. Katniss

2. Brutus hails from which District?

a. 2

b. 5

c. 7

d. 10

3. What is the name of Katniss' male tribute in the Hunger Games?

a. Haymitch

b. Gale

c. Peeta Mellark

d. Primrose Everdeen

4. What weapon does Katniss take from Glimmer?

a. Sword

b. Knife

c. Bow and Arrow

d. Shield

5. Lynn Cohen plays which character in Catching Fire?

a. Bags

b. Mags

c. Dags

d. Clags

6. The venom of what creature is used to "hijack" Peeta in Mocking Jay part 1?

a. Limpet

b. Tracker Jacker

c. Snape

d. Volocoraptor

7. Who attempted to stop Gale's whipping after 20 lashes?

a. Woof

b. Cray

c. Gale

d. Darius

8. Who directs The Hunger Game Mockingjay Part 2?

a. Simon Thomas

b. Damien Lewis

c. Andrew Morris

d. Francis Lawrence

9. Flavius is a prep team member of which character?

a. Katniss

b. Haymitch

c. Peeta

d. Effie

10. How is Thresh killed?

a. Wild Beasts

b. Katniss Bow

c. Drowning

d. Fire

11. Primrose is singled out by District 13 for what profession?

a. Law enforcement

b. Doctor

c. Soldier

d. President

12. From which district does Finnick Odair come form?

a. 4

b. 12

c. 14

d. 5

13. "Because of her, they all think they are invincible." Which character utters this line in Catching Fire?

a. President Snow

b. Haymitch

c. Plutrach

d. Gale

14. Axes are made in which District?

a. 7

b. 8

c. 1

d. 4

15. Who plays Johanna Mason in Catching Fire?

a. Willow Shields

b. Jennifer Lawrence

c. Elizabeth Banks

d. Jena Malone

16. What is Haymitchs surname?

a. Labernathy

b. Abernathy

c. Sabernathy

d. Cabernathy

17. "Haymitch, please. Please, just help me get through this trip." is a plea from which character in Catching Fire?

a. Katniss

b. President Snow

c. Plutrach

d. Gale

18. Katniss says Gale Hawthorne has what colour eyes in Catching Fire?

a. Blue

b. Grey

c. Red

d. Green

19. Nina Jacobson had what role in the first Hunger Games film?

a. Writer

b. Producer

c. Director

d. Actress

20. Who owned a cat named buttercup?

a. Katniss

b. Haymitch

c. Peeta

d. Primrose

Round 18

1. During a TV interview in Mockingjay, Peeta blurts out that which district is going to be attacked by Capitol?

a. 13

b. 4

c. 7

d. 9

2. Grain is the main industry of which District?

a. 9

b. 11

c. 12

d. 10

3. Which of the following Catching Fire actors has a star on the Hollywood Walk of Fame?

a. Soldier

b. Stanley Tucci

c. Woody Harrelson

d. Donald Sutherland

4. Ceciel and Woolf are victors from which District?

a. 8

b. 10

c. 3

d. 5

5. Which District does Katniss visit on her first stop of the Victory tour?

a. 14

b. 13

c. 11

d. 17

6. What is Annie's surname in Catching Fire?

a. Besta

b. Cresta

c. Desta

d. Vesta

7. How old is Mags in Catching Fire?

a. 80

b. 100

c. 60

d. 30

8. "There are much worse games to play" is the final line spoken by whom?

a. Katniss

b. Primrose

c. Finnick

d. Annie

9. Wes Chatham plays which character in Mockingjay Part 1?

a. Mastor

b. Castor

c. Pastor

d. Lastor

10. Where is the Capitol located?

a. Himalayas

b. Andres

c. Rocky Mountains

d. Everest

11. Which District was supposedly obliterated during the Dark Days?

a. 9

b. 11

c. 13

d. 6

12. Katniss Everdeen's name comes from a....?

a. Plant

b. Ocean

c. Rock

d. Animal

13. Which of these is the name of the song by Arcade Fire featured on The Hunger Games soundtrack?

a. Marys Baby

b. Moses Son

c. Josephs Wife

d. Abrahams Daughter

14. How many of the 12 Districts does Katniss visit on her victory tour in Catching Fire?

a. 12

b. 7

c. 3

d. 2

15. Who launches a vote in "Mockingjay" aimed at eliminating leaders children?

a. Haymitch

b. Peeta

c. Gale

d. Coin

16. What is the first name of Mr. Quaid who plays Marvel?

a. John

b. Jack

c. James

d. Jesse

17. What is name of the nation in which the series takes place?

a. Danem

b. Panem

c. Lanem

d. Sanem

18. Where is Katniss taken at the start of the Mockingjay film?

a. District 12

b. District 3

c. District 13

d. District 7

19. Who plays Peeta Mellark in The Hunger Games?

a. Liam Hemsworth

b. Lenny Kravitz

c. Woody Harrelson

d. Josh Hutchersn

20. Who utters the line "I don't care if we're rich, I just want you to come home"?

a. Katniss

b. Haymitch

c. Peeta

d. Primrose

Round 19

1. "I agree she should die but in the right way. At the right time. Katniss Everdeen is a symbol.". Which character speaks this line in Catching Fire?

a. Plutarch

b. Katniss

c. Primrose Everdeen

d. Haymitch

2. Mags and Annie hail from which District?

a. 6

b. 4

c. 1

d. 9

3. Which District has Coal as its main industry?

a. 6

b. 4

c. 12

d. 8

4. Snow murdered which of Haymitch's relatives after he won the Hunger Games?

a. Father

b. Mother

c. Brother

d. Sister

5. What is the occupation of Plutarch Heavensbee?

a. Miner

b. Soldier

c. Judge

d. Commentator

6. Who blurts out during a TV interview in Mocking Jay Part 1 that the Capitol is planning to attack District 13?

a. Primrose

b. Katniss

c. Coin

d. Peeta

7. Who plays Haymitch Abernathy in The Hunger Games?

a. Liam Hemsworth

b. Stanley Tucci

c. Josh Hutcherson

d. Woody Harrelson

8. Enobaria comes from which District?

a. 2

b. 1

c. 6

d. 9

9. How old is Primrose when she is killed?

a. 13

b. 23

c. 45

d. 33

10. What is the name of Katniss Everdeen's sister who she volunteers to replace on Reaping Day?

a. Scarlett

b. Violet

c. Primrose

d. Petal

11. Wilbur Fitzgerald plays which character in the movie?

a. Hay

b. Dray

c. Gray

d. Cray

12. The actor Afemo Omilami plays the Mayor of which district in Catching Fire?

a. 8

b. 11

c. 7

d. 10

13. What is the "industry" of District 5?

a. Money

b. Greed

c. Power

d. Influence

14. Devil May Cry is a song on the Catching Fire soundtrack by which band?

a. The Weekend

b. The Lumineers

c. The National

d. Coldplay

15. What is Annie's surname in Mockingjay Part 1?

a. Desta

b. Cresta

c. Festa

d. Mesta

16. What does President Snow say is the only thing stringer than fear?

a. Joy

b. Hope

c. Love

d. Romance

17. Who plays Wiress in Catching Fire?

a. Jena Malone

b. Meta Golding

c. Lynn Cohen

d. Amanda Plummer

18. What is the name of the song by Christina Aguilera that features on the soundtrack of Catching Fire?

a. We Regin

b. We Are

c. We Remain

d. We Rule

19. Which edition of The Hunger Games did Enobaria win?

a. 32

b. 42

c. 52

d. 62

20. Thresh hails fro which district?

a. 12

b. 11

c. 3

d. 4

Round 20

1. What role does Willow Shields play in Catching Fire?

a. Danem Everdeen

b. Katniss Everdeen

c. Primrose Everdeen

d. Petula Everdeen

2. Which role did Alan Edward Bell have in Catching Fire?

a. Director

b. Cinematographer

c. Composer

d. Editor

3. What is the main industry of District 6?

a. Mining

b. Fishing

c. Transportation

d. Farming

4. What colour does Cinna dress Katniss in in The Hunger Games?

a. Blue

b. Black

c. Gold

d. White

5. Where is Panem?

a. Asia

b. South America

c. North America

d. Europe

6. What relationship is Primrose Everdeen to Katniss?

a. Mother

b. Cousin

c. Sister

d. Daughter

7. Where does President Snow live?

a. District 2

b. District 1

c. Capitol

d. District 12

8. What is the time period known as, approx 75 years, before The Hunger Games?

a. Darkness Days

b. Nigt Days

c. Dark Days

d. Light Days

9. Which Districts main industry in Lumber?

a. 10

b. 4

c. 9

d. 7

10. What is the name of Gale Hawthorne's mother?

a. Henrietta

b. Harriet

c. Hazzelle

d. Hannah

11. Who is filmed signing The Hanging Tree in Mockingjay?

a. Peeta

b. Primrose

c. Haymitch

d. Katniss

12. Which of these is real character from the movies?

a. Lucky Sae

b. Tease Sae

c. Messy Sae

d. Greasy Sae

13. What nationality is hunger games author Suzanne Collins?

a. Canadian

b. English

c. American

d. French

14. Which Jennifer plays Katniss Everdeen in Catching Fire?

a. Smith

b. Aniston

c. Banks

d. Lawrence

15. Which character interviews competitors on Tv the night before Hunger Games contests?

a. Katniss Everdeen

b. Effie Trinket

c. Caesar Flickerman

d. Cinna

16. Which is the poorest District in Panem?

a. 6

b. 3

c. 4

d. 12

17. Who We Are is a song on the soundtrack by which band?

a. Coldplay

b. The Lumineers

c. The National

d. Imagine Dragons

18. Which other character has 2 children with Katniss?

a. Annie

b. Primrose

c. Finnick

d. Peeta

19. Which of these is a real character in The Hunger Games?

a. Tigerface

b. Funface

c. Vixenface

d. Foxface

20. Electronics is the main industry of which District?

a. 3

b. 1

c. 6

d. 8

Round 21

1. How often does The Hunger Games event take place in Panem?

a. Every Year

b. Every 2 Years

c. Every 3 Years

d. Every 4 Years

2. Who is Katniss reunited with in the opening of Mockingjay?

a. Ednis

b. Peeta

c. Haymitch

d. Primrose

3. Finnick is killed in which novel?

a. Mockingjay

b. The Hunger Games

c. Catching Fire

d. None

4. What colour eyes is Annie Cresta said to have?

a. Blue

b. Green

c. Brown

d. Red

5. Bogg is killed in what novel?

a. Mockingjay

b. The Hunger Games

c. Catching Fire

d. None

6. What is said that President Snows breath smells of?

a. Cheese

b. Blood

c. Garlic

d. Honey

7. Who suffers flashbacks towards the end of "Mockingjay"?

a. Annie

b. Primrose

c. Finnick

d. Peeta

8. What do Peeta and Katniss do in "Mockingjay" to preserve memories?

a. Shoot a Video

b. Write a Book

c. Post Online

d. Time Capsule

9. Which district does Gale in over in "Mockingjay" with his controversial strategy?

a. 8

b. 6

c. 2

d. 13

10. What is the first weapon Katniss gets in the her first battle in the Hunger Games?

a. Bow

b. Gun

c. Knife

d. Cannon

11. Where does Katniss say her goodbyes in the Hunger Games?

a. Café

b. School

c. Justice Building

d. Pub

12. From which district does Clove come from?

a. 2

b. 5

c. 9

d. 11

13. What is the main industry of District 3?

a. Food

b. Masonary

c. Electronics

d. Wine

14. Stephanie Schlund plays which role in Catching Fire?

a. Brutus

b. Cashmere

c. Wiress

d. Mags

15. How many people take part in The Hunger Games event?

a. 24

b. 48

c. 77

d. 12

16. Which District is home to Annie Cresta?

a. 3

b. 9

c. 4

d. 12

17. What colour is effuse hair?

a. Green

b. Pink

c. Black

d. Red

18. Which of these is a former Hunger Games winner?

a. Snow

b. Primrose

c. Effie

d. Haymitch

19. Who writes a book with Katniss in "Mockingjay"?

a. Annie

b. Primrose

c. Finnick

d. Peeta

20. Finnick is the lover of whom?

a. Annie

b. Katniss

c. Peeta

d. Prim

Round 22

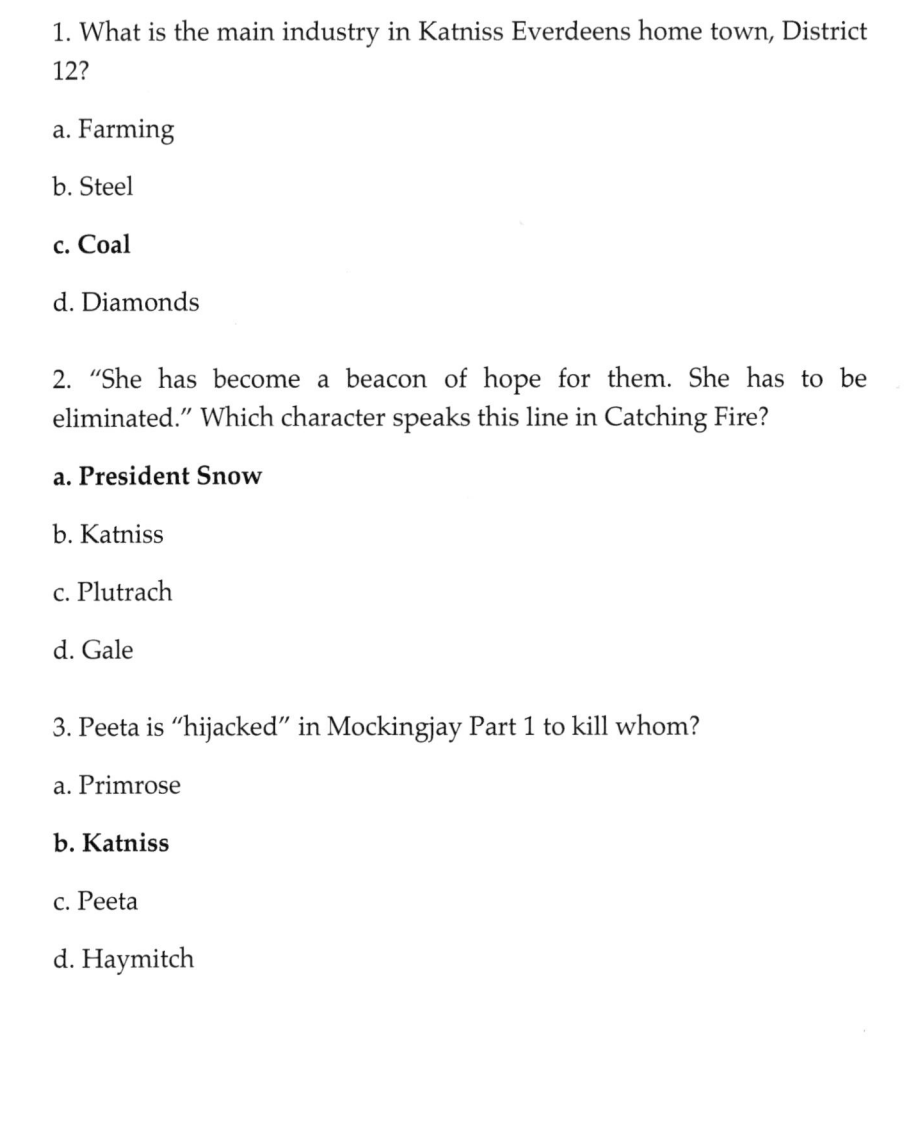

1. What is the main industry in Katniss Everdeens home town, District 12?

a. Farming

b. Steel

c. Coal

d. Diamonds

2. "She has become a beacon of hope for them. She has to be eliminated." Which character speaks this line in Catching Fire?

a. President Snow

b. Katniss

c. Plutrach

d. Gale

3. Peeta is "hijacked" in Mockingjay Part 1 to kill whom?

a. Primrose

b. Katniss

c. Peeta

d. Haymitch

4. What is Peeta's surname in The Hunger Games?

a. Bellark

b. Mellark

c. Sellark

d. Fellark

5. What is the first name of President Snow?

a. Careerin

b. Carin

c. Coriolanus

d. Carl

6. How many lashes did Gale receive before Darius tried to stop it?

a. 20

b. 40

c. 60

d. 80

7. Rue draws Katniss attention to what kind of creatures in The Hunger Games?

a. Lacker Fackers

b. Tracker Jackers

c. Sacker Whackers

d. Macker Jackers

8. Masonary is the industry of which District?

a. 3

b. 2

c. 4

d. 5

9. Where is District 7 located?

a. The East

b. The South

c. The North

d. The West

10. How much did Mockingjay part 1 take at the Box Office?

a. $752 million

b. $222 million

c. $2 billion

d. $10 million

11. Plutrach takes Katniss to the ruins of which area to convince her to join District 13's rebellion?

a. 3

b. 12

c. 4

d. 8

12. Which one of these is the name of a character who attacks Peeta in Mockingjay Part 1?

a. Coggs

b. Doggs

c. Foggs

d. Boggs

13. Haymictch comes from which district?

a. 12

b. 10

c. 8

d. 7

14. Enobaria is played by which actress in Catching Fire?

a. Meta Golding

b. Lynn Cohen

c. Jena Malone

d. Jennifer Lawrence

15. Bonnie and Twill hail from which district?

a. 8

b. 5

c. 3

d. 9

16. Plutarch Heavensbee is portrayed in the film by which actor?

a. Toby Jones

b. Phillip Seymour Hoffman

c. Donald Sutherland

d. Stanley Tucci

17. District 4 is known for which industry?

a. Fishing

b. Mining

c. Farming

d. Masonary

18. Julianne Moore plays which character in Mockingjay Part 1?

a. President Coin

b. President Snow

c. Annie

d. Boggs

19. What edition of the Hunger Games was won by Haymitch Abernathy?

a. 75th

b. 50th

c. 100th

d. 25th

20. What role does Lenny Kravitz play in the Hunger Games?

a. Dinna

b. Sinna

c. Cinna

d. Binna

Round 23

1. What does Katniss pick up in her first action at the start of the games?

a. Bow

b. Supplies

c. Gun

d. Arrow

2. The two runaways from district 8 tell Katniss they don't believe which District was wiped out in Catching Fire?

a. 20

b. 13

c. 21

d. 99

3. Which character becomes an Avox?

a. Davinia

b. Bavinia

c. Lavinia

d. Savinia

4. Woody Harrelson was born in which year?

a. 1981

b. 1971

c. 1951

d. 1961

5. Which of these characters is known as something of an inventor?

a. Woof

b. Haymitch

c. Cray

d. Beetee

6. How old is Foxface?

a. 15

b. 21

c. 33

d. 65

7. Peeta throws who to the wild beasts?

a. Mato

b. Cato

c. Plato

d. Dato

8. Which director left the Catching Fire project in April 2012?

a. Barry Ross

b. Ross Garry

c. Gary Ross

d. Ross Barry

9. Where does Gale work in Catching Fire?

a. Farming

b. Bakery

c. Mines

d. Arena

10. Which District has agriculture as its main industry?

a. 2

b. 14

c. 11

d. 6

11. What is the first name of Finnicks wife?

a. Dawn

b. Annie

c. Jessica

d. Elizabeth

12. What does President Snow where in his pocket to seemingly disguise the smell of his breath in Catching Fire?

a. A Yellow Flower

b. A White Rose

c. A Red Rose

d. A Purple Heart

13. What is the main industry of District 12?

a. Textiles

b. Grain

c. Coal

d. Lumber

14. What is Beetee's nickname?

a. Blimpy

b. Volts

c. Mental

d. Power

15. What occupation does Cinna have in Catching Fire?

a. Soldier

b. Cook

c. Stylist

d. Nurse

16. On Reaping day, 1 male and 1 female are chosen between what ages?

a. 11 to 16

b. 12 to 18

c. 10 to 14

d. 18 to 21

17. Who plays Beetee in Catching Fire?

a. Donald Sutherland

b. Sam Clafin

c. Toby Jones

d. Jeffrey Wright

18. In what environment is the 75th Edition of the Hunger Games held?

a. Jungle

b. Beach

c. Desert

d. Swamp

19. What is the name of the President of Panem?

a. President Rain

b. President Sun

c. President Snow

d. President Storm

20. Peeta Mellark comes from which District?

a. 13

b. 12

c. 10

d. 8

Round 24

1. Which of these animals poison Katniss in The Hunger Games?

a. Sacker Whackers

b. Macker Fackers

c. Lacker Mackers

d. Tracker Jackers

2. Wiress hails from which District?

a. 11

b. 4

c. 12

d. 3

3. Which district is home to Glimmer?

a. 6

b. 3

c. 1

d. 9

4. What is the surname of the character Romulus?

a. Bead

b. Dread

c. Thread

d. Dead

5. Which one of the following is a brother of Gale Hawthorne?

a. Ed

b. Nick

c. Frank

d. Vick

6. Who does Jennifer Lawrence play in the Hunger Games?

a. Gale

b. President Snow

c. Primrose Everdeen

d. Katniss

7. Where are Gales scars from his whipping from Capitol?

a. Chest

b. Legs

c. Back

d. Hands

8. What is Seneca's surname?

a. Everdeen

b. Crane

c. Flickerman

d. Foxface

9. How many districts comprise Panem?

a. 12

b. 14

c. 17

d. 21

10. What is the surname of Gale as played by Liam Hemsworth?

a. Hodgson

b. Harris

c. Hawthorne

d. Hillier

11. "Last year was child's play. This year, you're dealing with all experienced killers." is a line spoken by which character in Catching Fire?

a. Haymitch

b. President Snow

c. Plutrach

d. Gale

12. Who plays Mags in Catching Fire?

a. Elizabeth Banks

b. Jena Malone

c. Jennifer Lawrence

d. Lynn Cohen

13. Who tries to convince Peeta to eat deadly Nightlock in The Hunger Games?

a. Snow

b. Crane

c. Primrose Everdeen

d. Katniss

14. In what environment is the 75th Edition of the Hunger Games held?

a. Jungle

b. Beach

c. Desert

d. Swamp

15. Who directed the first Hunger Games movie?

a. Mark Anthony

b. Ross Smith

c. Gary Jones

d. Gary Ross

16. What character does Woody Harrelson play in the Hunger Games?

a. Gale

b. Haymitch

c. Primrose Everdeen

d. President Snow

17. Jon Kilk has what role in Catching Fire?

a. Producer

b. Composer

c. Director

d. Screenwriter

18. What genre would the Catching Fire movie fall into?

a. Comedy

b. Fantasy

c. Horror

d. Documentary

19. Mahershal Ali plays which character in Mockingjay Part 1?

a. Troggs

b. Boggs

c. Foggs

d. Coggs

20. Where is Nuclear Weaponry made?

a. District 9

b. District 10

c. District 13

d. District 1

Round 25

1. What is District 1 known for making?

a. Rice

b. Luxury Items

c. Corn

d. Milk

2. What is the first name of Gale Hawthorne's sister?

a. Dosy

b. Posy

c. Rosy

d. Cosy

3. Which one of the following is the correct name for a screenwriter for Catching Fire?

a. Daniel Arndt

b. David Arndt

c. Simon Arndt

d. Michael Arndt

4. Patina Miller plays which character in Mockingjay Part 1?

a. Commander Daylor

b. Commander Paylor

c. Commander Saylor

d. Commander Laylor

5. "We have to go Gale, before they kill us. They will kill us." is a line spoken by which character in Catching Fire?

a. Katniss

b. President Snow

c. Plutrach

d. Gale

6. Who unexpectedly attacks Katniss towards the end of Mockingjay Part 1?

a. Haymitch

b. Primrose

c. President Coin

d. Peeta

7. Who helps Katniss when she is poisoned by Tracker Jackers?

a. Fue

b. Sue

c. Mue

d. Rue

8. Who smiles at Katniss, just prior to being shot with a bow, that prevents her from doing so?

a. Peeta

b. Coin

c. Annie

d. Snow

9. Katniss agrees to the "mockingjay" if she gets the chance to kill whom?

a. President Snow

b. Primrose

c. Everdeen

d. Peeta

10. Where is Katniss sent after killing Coin in "Mockingjay"?

a. District 7

b. District 3

c. District 12

d. District 10

11. Which edition of The Hunger Games did Finnick Odair win?

a. 45th

b. 55th

c. 75th

d. 65th

12. Which character has notably pink hair?

a. Peeta

b. Haymitch

c. Effie

d. Katniss

13. What is the first name of Ms. Collins, author of Catching Fire?

a. Susan

b. Suzanne

c. Stella

d. Sally

14. Who is the escort of the District 12 Tributes?

a. Katniss

b. Haymitch

c. Peeta

d. Effie

15. Which district supplies Panem's peacekeepers?

a. 8

b. 5

c. 2

d. 1

16. President Snow sends White roses to District 13 in Mockingjay Part 1 to tease whom?

a. Primrose

b. Katniss

c. Peeta

d. President Coin

17. Darius tried to prevent who from being whipped after 20 lashes in Catching Fire?

a. Gale

b. Cray

c. Gale

d. Woof

18. Evan Ross plays which character in Mockingjay Part 1?

a. Messalla

b. Dessalla

c. Fessalla

d. Ressalla

19. Who plays the role of Cinna in the Hunger Games films?

a. Josh Hutcherson

b. Woody Harrelson

c. Stanley Tucci

d. Lenny Kravitz

20. Jo Williams has what role in Catching Fire?

a. Cinematographer

b. Composer

c. Director

d. Screenwriter

Thank you for using this book, I hope you have enjoyed it.

If you have enjoyed the book, please leave a review wherever you bought it - this will help other Hunger Games fans find and enjoy the book as much as you have!

Printed in Great Britain
by Amazon